At the Zoo

Written by
Alice Hemming

Yesterday we went to the zoo.

It was a long bus ride to get there.

At the zoo I saw a mother elephant and her baby. The baby elephant was so cute.

The elephants were friendly. I gave the mother elephant some food.

The kangaroos have big strong tails to help them jump.

I saw lots of new animals, too.

These are called dik-diks. They are tiny deer.

This is an aardvark. It has long pointy ears and it likes to eat ants.

The komodo dragons stuck out their tongues.

I liked the red panda best.

It climbed up into a tree. Then it rested in the sun.

It looked so cuddly
that I wanted to take it home.

We had our lunch near the otters.

Some ducks wanted our food!

Then we went to the playground.

I tried to swing like a monkey.

I ran and jumped like a dik-dik.

I climbed like a red panda.

I jumped and jumped along like a kangaroo.

I stuck out my tongue like a komodo dragon.

Then I felt worn out.

It was time to go home.

And I did take a red panda home with me!